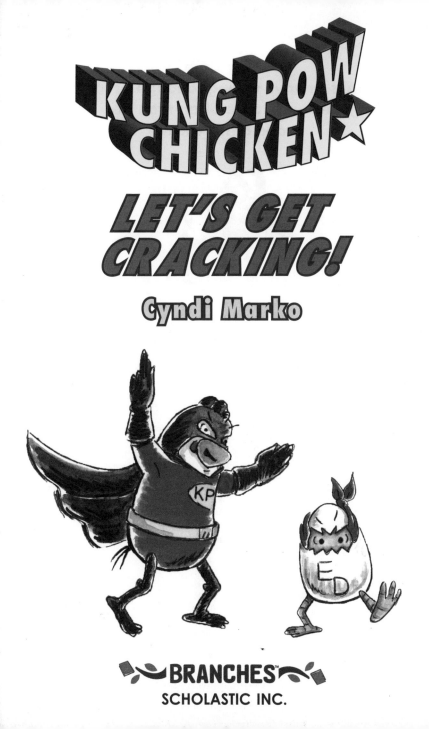

# KUNG POW CHICKEN★
## LET'S GET CRACKING!

### Cyndi Marko

BRANCHES

SCHOLASTIC INC.

# For Liam,
## who is always willing to laugh at my bad egg jokes and, more often than not, offer one of his own

Library of Congress Cataloging-in-Publication Data

Marko, Cyndi, author, illustrator.
Let's get cracking! / by Cyndi Marko.
pages cm. — (Kung Pow Chicken ; 1)
Summary: Gordon Blue and his brother Benny, unlikely superheroes, must save
Fowladelphia from Granny Goosebumps, who has filled the city with cookies that cause
innocent chickens' feathers to fall off.
ISBN 978-0-545-61062-9 (hardcover) — ISBN 978-0-545-61061-2 (pbk.) 1.
Superheroes—Juvenile fiction. 2. Chickens—Juvenile fiction. 3. Cookies—Juvenile fiction.
[1. Superheroes—Fiction. 2. Chickens—Fiction. 3. Cookies—Fiction. 4. Humorous stories.] I.
Title. II. Title: Let us get cracking.
PZ7.M33968Let 2014
813.6—dc23

2013018130

12 11 10 9 8 7 6 5 4 3 2 1                                    14 15 16 17 18 19/0

Printed in China                                                                 38

First Scholastic printing, January 2014

# TABLE OF CONTENTS

superhero poster

ROCKET ROOSTER

supersonic rocket

bunny slippers

drum

Gordon Blue seemed like an ordinary chicken.

Gordon was in second grade at an ordinary school.

He lived in an ordinary house in the ordinary city of Fowladelphia. But he had a <u>super</u> secret.

Only Uncle Quack and Gordon's younger
brother, Benedict, knew Gordon's secret.
Uncle Quack was a scientist. He worked
in a lab.

One day when Gordon and Benny were
younger, they had visited Uncle Quack
at work.

Gordon and Benny started playing Follow
the Leader. Gordon was in the lead and Benny
followed every move Gordon made. Then . . .

. . . Gordon tripped and fell into a huge vat of
bubbling toxic sludge! Benny followed Gordon's
lead.

Uncle Quack quickly rescued his nephews.

But later Gordon started to feel strange. And as time passed he felt even stranger.

He tingled when
danger was near.

He flapped his wings like the wind.

And he crowed louder than other chickens.
His bok was worse than his bite.

Gordon was no longer just an ordinary chicken. The toxic sludge had given him superpowers.

So Gordon made a super suit.

And Gordon came up with a super name:

Gordon promised to use his powers to right wrongs, to fight bad guys, and to keep his room <u>super</u> clean.

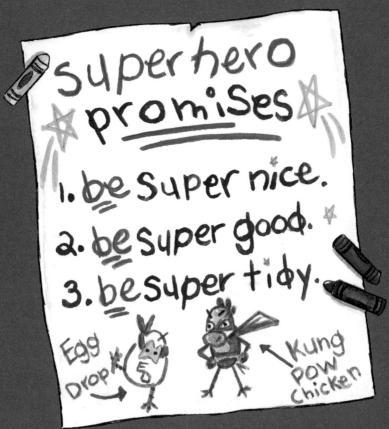

But Gordon hadn't met any bad guys yet. So he still had to do ordinary chicken things, like go to school.

Today was a bright fall day and Gordon was <u>super</u> excited about the school field trip to the Fowl Fall Festival.

Gordon's mother straightened his school tie and handed him his lunch box.

Gordon carried his lunch box everywhere. But he never let anyone see what was inside.

Mrs. Blue gave Gordon her very best mom stare. Gordon put on the hat.

Before her kids could escape, Mrs. Blue looped a scarf around Benny. Then she covered both Gordon and Benny in kisses.

Gordon and Benny walked to school.

When Gordon and Benny got to school, they joined their classmates out front. Everyone was excited to go to the Fowl Fall Festival.

Finally, the school bus arrived.

When they got to the festival, Gordon's teacher, Mr. Giblets, gave a long talk about rules.

. . . No pecking or shoving
bok, bok, bok . . .
stay with your buddy
bok, bok, bok . . . best behavior
bok, bok, bok . . .

Gordon and Benny were ready to burst. Gordon wanted to see the magician. Benny wanted to eat candy corn. And they both wanted to have a cookie.

Then Gordon's beak started to twitch. And his tail feathers began to wiggle.

Gordon could tell something was wrong, <u>very</u> wrong.

My birdy senses are tingling. . . . Someone must be up to no good!

Gordon and Benny pushed through the large flock of chickens. They were on the lookout for bad guys.

Suddenly, clucks and feathers filled the air. Gordon stared open-beaked. Everywhere he looked, feathers were blasting off chickens with a loud POOF!

POOF!

BOK!

I've got chickenbumps!

POOF!

Don't you mean goosebumps? Chickenbumps isn't a word!

But I'm a chicken and I have bumps!

BOK!

POOF!

They dashed inside. Gordon flung open his
lunch box. . . .

A few seconds later, Kung Pow Chicken and his sidekick, Egg Drop, burst into action!

**LET'S GET CRACKING!**

**HI-YAH!**

The heroes looked high and low for any sign of the bad guys. Then they spotted a busy booth selling hand-knit sweaters. Chilly naked chickens were scrambling to buy the sweaters.

My birdy senses are doing the Funky Chicken! That granny must be up to no good!

Kung Pow Chicken sneaked in for a closer look.

But he was spotted!

Egg Drop stopped. He dropped. And he rolled like thunder. . . .

Kung Pow Chicken burst free of the tangled trap. He flashed his Drumsticks of Doom!

I'm Kung Pow Chicken! You are <u>doomed</u> to go to jail!

KAPOW!

Granny Goosebumps used her Naughty Knitting Needles to fling yarn at Kung Pow Chicken. He plucked the spinning yarn out of the air with his drumsticks. Then he became locked in a battle of knits with the grumpy granny.

Granny Goosebumps threw Kung Pow Chicken to the ground.

Suddenly, some other grannies came crashing through the crowd. They scooped up Granny Goosebumps and sped away!

On the bus ride home, Gordon didn't want to talk. Outside, the city itched for a hero.

As soon as Gordon got home, he went straight to his room.

He put on his favorite bunny slippers.

He snuggled under his favorite blanket.

And he read his favorite comic book.

Benny knocked on Gordon's door.

Sigh.

Gordon, you have to get up!

No way! I can't do it. I tried. I'm just not a hero.

Ham and eggs, Gordon! You're a superhero! If _you_ won't fight bad guys, who will?

Gordon knew Benny was right. He needed to be brave because the city needed his help. And no crummy cookie or grumpy granny was going to stop him. He grabbed his lunch box.

I am Kung Pow Chicken . . . and Granny Goosebumps had better mind her manners.

Gordon and Benny found their mother in the kitchen.

Gordon and Benny hopped on their Big Wheel.
They rode up and down the streets. Every
chicken they passed wore an itchy sweater
and a sad face. Feathers and
cookie crumbs covered
the ground.

ITCH

ITCH

97

99

10

Gordon handed Uncle Quack a cookie. Uncle Quack looked at it very carefully. He turned it over. He gave it a sniff.

Then Uncle Quack popped the cookie in his mouth.

Gordon told Uncle Quack all about Granny Goosebumps and what had happened at the Fowl Fall Festival.

Gordon and Benny ran to their Big Wheel.

Gordon and Benny zoomed away from the lab. They were headed back to the Fowl Fall Festival to look for clues. They had to find Granny Goosebumps.

Gordon and Benny parked the Big Wheel under a tree. There wasn't a chicken in sight. So Gordon let his birdy senses lead the way . . .

. . . and he fell flat on his face. Sometimes
Gordon's birdy senses were a pain in the beak.
When he opened his eyes, he spotted a clue!

Benny picked up the clue. He took a
closer look.

Gordon and Benny ducked behind a bush. . . .

Kung Pow Chicken and Egg Drop jumped out,
ready to kick Granny Goosebumps in the tail
feathers!

Kung Pow Chicken pressed a button on his Beak-Phone.

The Big Wheel turned into the Beak-Mobile. Kung Pow Chicken pedaled it at top speed.

The superheroes drove to the address on
the card.

A granny in a pink housecoat and fuzzy slippers opened the door.

The granny went to get candies for the trick-or-treaters. While her back was turned, Kung Pow Chicken and Egg Drop ran past her and into the building.

They tiptoed down empty hallway,
after empty hallway,
after empty hallway.

The emptiness was spooky. Finally, the heroes
turned a corner and heard a scary sound.

Kung Pow Chicken gave Egg Drop a boost so he could peek inside.

Egg Drop leaned forward to get a better look.
The door fell open. Kung Pow Chicken and Egg
Drop both tumbled into the room.

SWOOSH!

Um,
trick or treat?

ZOING!

Granny Goosebumps, you're one bad egg!

Thank you, dearie!
Yes, soon my cookies will be all over the city. Every chicken will be naked and cold. They'll <u>need</u> to buy my sweaters! Then I'll have lots of money! And I can finally move to Florida!

Kung Pow Chicken and Egg Drop struggled and strained against the yarn. It was no use. They were wrapped up tight.

Kung Pow Chicken's beak trembled. He shrank away from the glowing cookie. Then the Beak-Phone rang.

RIINNG!

Kung Pow Chicken squiggled under the yarn. He popped his phone through the strands. It was his mother calling.

You boys are late for dinner! You are both in **BIG** trouble!!

That did it. Granny Goosebumps had made Kung Pow Chicken late for dinner. He was mad! It was time to show this bad granny who wore the leotard. It was time to be a superhero. He sucked in a super breath and —

BOK!

KICK!

You'll do your knitting behind bars now, Granny Goosebumps! Fowladelphia doesn't want your itchy sweaters. And we have the city's biggest brain working on how to regrow feathers!

RRRIINNNG! 🎵 🎵

Boys? It's Uncle Quack! Get to the lab **NOW**!

We're on our way!

Mom's going to be so mad.

Uncle Quack had created a glowy milk. He had dunked himself in it and now his feathers were back fuller than ever! But he didn't know how to get the milk to all the other naked chickens.

Granny Goosebumps had been caught, and the naked chickens were about to regrow their feathers. Kung Pow Chicken and Egg Drop could be ordinary chickens again.

Benny, I'm stuck! Help me get this leotard off!

Whose idea was it for superheroes to wear leotards, anyway?

Gordon and Benny joined Uncle Quack's
pool party. Soon, all of the naked chickens
had been dunked in the pool of glowy milk.
They showed off their fine new feathers.

POOF!

POOF!

POOF!

POOF!

POOF!

Feather Gro™

You can thank
Kung Pow Chicken
for your new
feathers!

Gordon and Benny rode home as fast as
Gordon's chicken legs could go.
Mrs. Blue met them at the door.

Gordon and Benedict
Blue! I should take away
your Big Wheel!

But Uncle Quack called and
said you had dinner at the
lab. And he said you helped
those poor naked chickens
I saw on the news!

<u>So</u> you're not in trouble.
But next time, you had
better call me!

We will, Mom.

Hmmph. It's not <u>my</u>
fault. I can't even
have a phone!

Then she gave them both a kiss and sent
them off to bed.

Gordon and Benny sat on Gordon's bed. They talked about everything that had happened that day. Gordon was proud to finally be a <u>real</u> superhero.

Suddenly, Gordon's tail feathers began to wiggle.

second grade photo →

← tiara

**Cyndi Marko** lives in Canada with her family. She wears a lot of itchy sweaters.

When Cyndi was in second grade, her teacher said her printing was too messy and that she had to practice more. But instead of practicing printing after school, Cyndi would slip into her Wonder Woman costume and red rubber boots. Then she would pedal her purple tricycle around the block at top speed, fighting bad guys! Although Cyndi has since given up crime fighting, she still has messy printing. (Sorry, Mrs. Sieffert!)

Kung Pow Chicken is Cyndi's first children's book series.

lasso →

wrist cuffs

← red rubber boots

← purple tricycle

# KUNG POW CHICKEN ★

**Prove your superhero know-how!**

How did Gordon and Benny get superpowers?

How does Gordon know when danger is near?

What is Granny Goosebumps's evil plan? And how do Gordon and Benny save the day?

How is Kung Pow Chicken similar to superheroes in other stories?

Give yourself a superhero name, draw your costume, and write about why you want to be a superhero.

scholastic.com/branches